THE GHOST OF DONLEY FARM

by Jaime Gardner Johnson
illustrated by Laurie Allen Klein

Rebecca, the red-tailed hawk, had the perfect home. It was an open grassland area with a few scattered trees where she had a good view in all directions. She could see the golden wheat fields, the green meadows, and the shiny blue water from ponds. Her favorite place to sit was on an old wooden fence alongside the Donley Farm. From here, she was always sure to spot a mouse or two scurrying through the tall thistle and ragweed. It was the perfect habitat for a hawk.

There was not a part of the Donley Farm Rebecca had not explored. She knew every mole hole in the grass fields, every prickly Osage orange tree that lined the farm property, and even the buzzard clan that roosted in the ancient white oak tree behind the homestead. But there was one thing Rebecca had never seen, and that was the famous barn ghost of the Donley Farm.

Rebecca had heard that this ghost was nocturnal. Nocturnal animals come out only at night, unlike Rebecca. She was diurnal and active during the day. She wanted to see if this ghost really existed. She would need to stay up past the setting sun, and explore when the Big Dipper could finally be seen in the dark, open sky.

Was she scared? Of course not! Rebecca knew that her sharp talons and her pointy, curved beak made her one of the fiercest raptors of the sky.

The fields were starting to get dark with the rising moon. Fireflies began to sprinkle light first here, then there, all across the grassland. Bullfrogs at the pond made music together. *Riiiiiiiiiiiiibit. Riiiiiiiiiiiibit.* The air was chilly and wet. Night had come.

"*Screeeeeeeeeeeeeeeeeech*!" What was that? Rebecca heard a terrifying noise. It came from the creaky, old barn. Rebecca was sure that the ghost had made the noise. She immediately took off to find out for herself.

As she approached the dark and scary barn, she began to wonder if she should turn around. Should she fly back to her safe resting spot in the old maple tree? She was a mighty creature of the sky, but the screeching howl from the dark barn made her shiver with fright.

She flew to a small open window and looked into the barn. Sure enough, a white figure was in the corner. She tried to see the ghost more clearly, but she could not see in the dark. Her eyesight was much better during the day. The ghost, however, noticed her and quietly came closer. Rebecca was suddenly scared, even with her sharp talons and pointy beak. The ghost moved closer without making a single sound. Rebecca saw that it had two legs, a beak, wings to help it fly, and most importantly, feathers. A bird, just like her! It had sharp talons and a sharp, curved beak. Like her, it was a raptor, a meat-eating bird of prey.

"What are you doing here in my house?" asked the strange ghost bird.

"I b-b-beg your pardon," Rebecca whispered back, "but I wanted to see if there really was a ghost living in Donley's barn."

"Hahahaha!" laughed the white, glowing animal. "I am not a ghost, can't you see? I am a bird. I have been called a ghost my whole life, but I'd rather be called a barn owl. My name is Bernard."

Suddenly Rebecca felt silly for being afraid of another bird! But, she still didn't understand why she had never met Bernard. "But why don't you come out and fly during the day, like all the other normal animals?" Rebecca asked, trying not to be rude. She was thinking about the singing bluebirds, the slithering garter snakes, and the buzzing bees that came out during the day.

"I was wondering the same thing about you," responded Bernard. Rebecca seemed confused, so Bernard said, "All of the animals I know are out and about at night. For example, Silas the smelly skunk. Or big-eared Bart, the brown bat. And don't forget about my favorite snack, the delicious field voles."

"Silas the smelly skunk? I've never heard of him, or smelled him!"

"Of course you've never smelled him! Most birds cannot smell very much." They both laughed because it was true. Their beaks were good for tearing meat, but they were not like noses. They could smell nothing.

"I see Silas every now and again, and I sure can hear him before he is even in sight," Bernard continued. Rebecca laughed again. She also had an excellent sense of hearing. She was often surprised at how loud the other animals were when they ran in the field or flapped their wings overhead. Even when these animals tried to be quiet, Rebecca could easily hear them making noise.

"But how do you see Silas?" asked Rebecca in amazement. "I can barely see you, and you are only a few feet away and all white!"

"Really?" Bernard asked. He was very surprised. "I can see you perfectly," he added.

At first Rebecca did not believe Bernard. She took a closer look at his eyes. Bernard had enormous eyes! They were like two big brown eggs bulging from his soft feathers.

"But how on earth do you see during the day?" Bernard asked. "The bright sun burns my eyes and everything is blurry."

"Oh, I can see fantastically well in the day," Rebecca proudly declared, regaining her confidence. "I can see the red glimmer of the ruby-throated hummingbird, the orange scales of the fluttering monarch, and the blue blossoms of the chicory along the road."

"Color!" exclaimed Bernard. "My eyes help me see shapes at night, but I do not see colors."

"And anyway," Rebecca added, "the sun does not bother me so much because I have a ridge over my eyes that helps block out the bright light." Bernard looked closely at her face and noticed that it was true. Rebecca had a long bump over her eyes. His face was flat like a disk, except for his bulging egg-like eyes.

Blink. Blink. Rebecca was not used to being up so late and was getting sleepy. She started to struggle to keep all three eyelids open. When she opened all three back up, Bernard was gone!

"Bernard," she whispered. "Bernard!" she shouted a little louder. He had flown away without her even hearing a sound. "*Humph!* He must be hungry and off to find some food," thought Rebecca. "But how did he fly away so silently without my noticing? Perhaps it was those soft feathers that cover his whole body, even his legs!" Rebecca looked at her own feathers. They were not as soft, and they made noise when she flapped in the wind. But, her rigid feathers helped her to soar high in the sky.

Then she looked at her bare, scaly legs and shivered. "*Brrrrrrr*. Night sure is chilly! I wish my legs were more like Bernard's and covered with feathers!" Then she remembered how hot the sun could be on her scaly legs during the day. She was happy her legs were bare. She would surely be too hot with feathery legs on a sunny day.

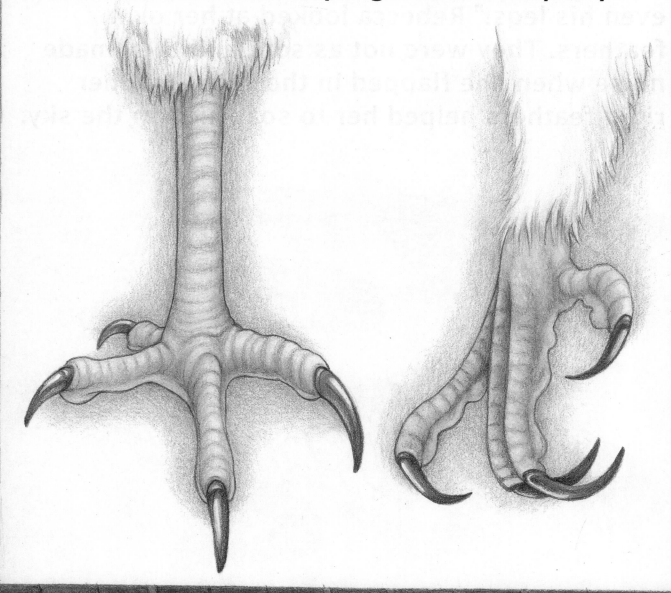

"I think Bernard is a wise, old owl for hunting at night," thought Rebecca. "After all, he can see and hear better in the night, he can fly silently, and he stays warm with his soft feathers in the cool evening air.

If we both hunted for food right now in the same field, one of us would go hungry. If I come out in the day, and he comes out at night, we never have to worry about competing with each other for food."

The thought of food made Rebecca realize that she needed rest. She had a big day of hunting tomorrow. And boy, was she tired. Rebecca decided it was time to fly back to her favorite resting spot in the red maple tree. It had broad branches for her to perch safely and thick leaves to block out the chilly sting of night. On windy nights, she could watch the helicopter seeds sputter through the air and across the field. They looked just like a bird flying.

Watching the maple seeds dance across the sky in the glow of the moon, Rebecca spotted a distant shape swooping, diving, plunging, sliding, and sweeping through the open air. She knew it was the ghost of the Donley Farm. He was looking for his own lunch in the busy night.

For Creative Minds

Diurnal or Nocturnal

Animals that are active during the day and asleep at night are diurnal. Animals that are active at night and asleep during the day are nocturnal. Read the following sentences and look for clues to determine if the animal is diurnal or nocturnal.

A large dog sneaks up on the **skunk** in the dark of night. The skunk stamps her feet and throws her tail up in the air. She gives the other animal a warning before spraying.

The **garter snake** passes the morning hunting and basking in the warm sunlight. If a predator arrives, he will hide his head under some leaves and flail his tail until it goes away.

This **bluebird** is a helpful garden bird. He spends his days eating insects off the plants and defending his territory from other birds.

The bright afternoon sun helps this high-flying **red-tailed hawk** search for her next meal. She can see a grasshopper from more than 200 feet (61m) away!

As night falls, a small, flying beetle with a glowing abdomen emerges. She flashes her light to signal to other **fireflies** to come out. Soon the field is glowing with their dancing lights.

The **barn owl** sweeps over the field under the dark night sky. He flies slowly and silently, scanning the ground for prey.

Answers. Diurnal: garter snake, bluebird, red-tailed hawk
Nocturnal: skunk, fireflies, barn owl

Raptor Diets

An animal's **diet** is all of the things that animal eats or drinks. Raptors like barn owls and red-tailed hawks are **carnivores**, which means they eat other animals. Red-tailed hawks live on a diet of mostly small mammals, but will also eat reptiles, birds, and even insects. Red-tailed hawks can hunt prey more than twice their size. Barn owls usually eat small rodents and other birds. Although they prefer rodents, barn owls will eat other animals as well, including bats, insects, and toads. Because barn owls hunt rodents, many farmers set up nesting boxes to encourage barn owls to live around their barn and keep the rodent population down.

Diurnal   Nocturnal

Raptor Fun Facts

A raptor is a bird that hunts and kills other animals for food. They can also be called birds of prey.

Raptors use their feet to grab onto their prey off the ground or snatch them out of midair. In fact, the word "raptor" comes from a Latin word, *rapare*, which means to grab, snatch, or carry off.

Most raptors are diurnal. Among raptors, only owls are nocturnal.

Because barn owls are nocturnal and red-tailed hawks are diurnal, they would not usually meet in the wild. Since they hunt at different times, they can share a territory and not compete with each other for food.

Barn owls live on six of the seven continents. The only continent where barn owls are not found is Antarctica.

Red-tailed hawks can reach speeds as fast as 120 miles (193km) per hour. Most birds have bones that are partly hollow. This makes the bird lighter and helps them to fly.

Red-tailed hawks live in many different habitats, including both wild areas and in regions where humans live.

Barn owls can swallow small prey whole. They later spit up the bones and other pieces of the animal that they cannot digest.

Raptor Adaptations

Owls and hawks are both raptors—birds who hunt and eat meat. Raptors are excellent predators because of special adaptations that help them hunt and catch their prey.

Both the red-tailed hawk and the barn owl have feathers that are adapted to help them hunt. The red-tailed hawk has long, stiff feathers that let her glide for a long time with very little effort. The barn owl has short, soft feathers that are completely silent in flight and allow him to sneak up on his prey.

Animals see by using sensory cells in their eyes, called rods and cones. Animals with many cones, like the red-tailed hawk, can see color clearly. Rods are sensitive to dim light and are best at detecting motion. Raptors have large eyes with many sensory cells that allow them to spot their prey from a great distance or in dim light.

Birds have three eyelids! Like humans, birds have an upper and a lower eyelid that close to block out light. A bird's third eyelid is see-through and closes from the side. This thin membrane protects the raptors' eyes from wind, water, dirt, and other debris. It also keeps the eyes moist so that the bird does not need to blink. This helps raptors keep their eyes focused on their prey during the hunt.

Talons are sharp claws on the raptors' feet that help them grab their prey. Owls use their feet and talons to squeeze their prey to death before eating them. Hawks have large talons that hold tight to squirming prey.

To my mother Margret Nancy Johnson, who fostered my love of the outdoors and encouraged me to write.—JGJ
For BK and JK, who make all things possible.—LAK
Thanks to Deb Oexmann, Director of Brukner Nature Center, for verifying the accuracy of the information in this book. The author donates a percentage of her royalties to Brukner Nature Center.

Library of Congress Cataloging-in-Publication Data from Library of Congress goes here...or

Cataloging Information is available through the Library of Congress:

9781628554519 English hardcover ISBN
9781628554595 English paperback ISBN
9781628554670 Spanish paperback ISBN
9781628554755 English eBook downloadable ISBN
9781628554830 Spanish eBook downloadable ISBN
Interactive, read-aloud eBook featuring selectable English (9781628554915) and Spanish (9781628554991) text and audio (web and iPad/tablet based) ISBN
LCCN: 2014011143

Translated into Spanish: El fantasma de la granja Donley
Lexile® Level: 750
key phrases for educators: adaptations, diurnal/nocturnal

Bibliography:

Dunn, Jon L, Jonathan K. Alderfer, and Paul E. Lehman. National Geographic Field Guide to the Birds of Eastern North America. Washington, D.C: National Geographic, 2008.
Thompson, Bill. The Young Birder's Guide to Birds of North America (Peterson Field Guides). Boston, MA: Houghton Mifflin Harcourt, 2012.
Zickefoose, Julie. The Bluebird Effect: Uncommon Bonds with Common Birds. Boston, MA: Houghton Mifflin Harcourt, 2012.

Text Copyright 2014 © by Jaime Gardner Johnson
Illustration Copyright 2014 © by Laurie Allen Klein

Manufactured in China, June 2014
This product conforms to CPSIA 2008
First Printing

Arbordale Publishing
Mt. Pleasant, SC 29464
www.ArbordalePublishing.com

CPSIA information can be obtained at www.ICGtesting.com
Printed in the USA
LVOW02s1143110514

385244LV00001B/14/P